A wind sprang up, whipping Isabel's curly hair around her face. She was spinning, Cloud's mane blowing up as they spiraled faster and faster. Isabel clung to Cloud as he suddenly plummeted down.

LOOK OUT FOR MORE
ADVENTURES AT

UNICORN ACADEMY

Sophia and Rainbow
Scarlett and Blaze
Ava and Star
Isabel and Cloud
Layla and Dancer
Olivia and Snowflake

★ ★ ★

UNICORN ACADEMY
Isabel and Cloud

JULIE SYKES
illustrated by LUCY TRUMAN

A STEPPING STONE BOOK™
Random House 🏠 New York

To Joanne Temple,
who always tells a good story

Text copyright © 2018 by Julie Sykes and Linda Chapman
Cover art and interior illustrations copyright © 2018 by Lucy Truman

All rights reserved. Published in the United States by Random House Children's Books, a division of Penguin Random House LLC, New York. Originally published in paperback in the United Kingdom by Nosy Crow Ltd, London, in 2018.

Random House and the colophon are registered trademarks and A Stepping Stone Book and the colophon are trademarks of Penguin Random House LLC.

Visit us on the Web! rhcbooks.com

Educators and librarians, for a variety of teaching tools,
visit us at RHTeachersLibrarians.com

Library of Congress Cataloging-in-Publication Data
Names: Sykes, Julie, author. | Truman, Lucy, illustrator.
Title: Isabel and Cloud / Julie Sykes; illustrated by Lucy Truman.
Description: First American edition. | New York: Random House, [2019]
| Series: Unicorn Academy; #4 | "A Stepping Stone Book." | Originally
published: London: Nosy Crow, 2018.
Summary: Isabel is having trouble getting along with other students, her
teachers, and even her unicorn, Cloud, but another threat to
Unicorn Academy brings them back together.
Identifiers: LCCN 2018035108 | ISBN 978-1-9848-5091-1 (pbk.) |
ISBN 978-1-9848-5092-8 (hardcover library binding) |
ISBN 978-1-9848-5093-5 (ebook)
Subjects: | CYAC: Unicorns—Fiction. | Magic—Fiction. | Friendship—
Fiction. | Boarding schools—Fiction. | Schools—Fiction.
Classification: LCC PZ7.S98325 Is 2019 | DDC [Fic]—dc23

Printed in the United States of America
10 9 8 7 6 5 4 3 2 1
First American Edition

"Try again." Isabel pointed at the bundle of twigs surrounded by stones. "You can do this, Cloud. And think what fun it would be to make a fire."

Cloud nuzzled her. "Okay, Isabel, I'll try again for you. But I'm almost certain that I don't have fire magic."

It was lunchtime at Unicorn Academy, and most students and their unicorns were lazing around together on the banks of Sparkle Lake, enjoying the summer sunshine. Isabel and her unicorn, Cloud, had sneaked away to a quieter part of the grounds.

"You don't know for sure." Isabel stroked Cloud's neck, tracing the pale-blue swirls on his white coat. "I think you just need to try harder."

All the unicorns on Unicorn Island were born with a special magic power, although they couldn't be sure when that power would be revealed. Isabel was desperate for Cloud to discover his magic.

Please let Cloud be like Blaze and have fire magic, she thought.

Blaze, Scarlett's unicorn, had been one of the first unicorns to discover her magic. Isabel was happy for Scarlett, her best friend, but she secretly hated the fact that Blaze had discovered her magic before Cloud.

Cloud stared intently at the pile of sticks. He lifted a hoof and struck the ground.

"Again!" instructed Isabel. "Do it again, harder. I'm sure there was a spark."

Cloud rapped the ground repeatedly. The noise made Isabel's ears ring, and the dusty earth made Cloud sneeze.

"Achoo!" Cloud couldn't stop sneezing. "Sorry, Isabel. I really can't make fire."

Isabel heaved a sigh. "Okay, well, maybe fire magic isn't your thing. Why don't you try turning invisible again? I'm sure the tip of your ear vanished the last time you tried."

Cloud shook his head. "No, it didn't, and I think

we should stop. My parents told me that magic can't be rushed. We both need to be patient."

Isabel buried her face in his silver-and-blue mane, trying to hide the frustration inside her. Cloud was lovely, he was sweet and kind, but Isabel couldn't help wondering if Ms. Primrose, the academy's head teacher, had made a mistake when she put them together. Ms. Primrose said that she paired students with the best unicorn for them, but patient Cloud wasn't anything like competitive Isabel.

Is he really the right unicorn for me? she thought. *Surely I should have a lively, more adventurous unicorn like Blaze.*

Like all the other first years, Isabel was ten years old and had started at Unicorn Academy back in January. The students spent at least a year at the school, getting to know their own special unicorn and learning how to become guardians of Unicorn Island. Their beautiful island was nourished by the magical multicolored water that flowed from the center of the earth and out through a fountain in Sparkle Lake in the grounds of Unicorn Academy. The water was then carried around the island by rivers and streams, and its magical properties helped people, animals, and plants to flourish.

Most students and unicorns only spent a year at Unicorn Academy, but some stayed longer. Ms. Primrose called them the lucky ones because they got extra time at the academy while their unicorns discovered their magic or bonded with their student. When a unicorn and student bonded, a lock of the student's hair turned the same color as their unicorn's mane.

"I need a rest," said Cloud. "Let's go back to the lake."

"Okay," said Isabel, vaulting onto his back.

She really hoped Cloud would discover his magic soon. She didn't think she could bear staying at Unicorn Academy another year, after all her friends had left!

They set off for Sparkle Lake. Isabel shaded her eyes from the dazzling sunshine as they drew nearer. She could see her friends from Sapphire dorm sitting exactly where she'd left them. The group was talking in whispers, casting glances at Sparkle Lake. Isabel had a feeling she knew what they were talking about.

"Someone's definitely trying to cause trouble," said Sophia as she threaded daisies together in a long chain. "Too many bad things have happened for it to be a coincidence." Sophia pushed her hair back over her shoulder. "There was the time the lake was polluted and the time when it froze over—"

"But who would try to harm the lake?"

interrupted Ava. "Everyone knows that nothing on Unicorn Island can flourish without its magical water." She had replaced the usual sprig of forget-me-nots in her chin-length hair with a red rose.

"I don't know, but whoever it was tried to harm our unicorns too," said Layla with a shiver. She

reached out to stroke her unicorn Dancer's nose. "Remember how they almost destroyed the sky-berry bushes?"

Sky berries grew on the mountains behind the school. They were the unicorns' favorite food, and more importantly, they were rich in the vitamins the unicorns needed to stay healthy.

"It's really scary," said Sophia. "I wish we could do something to help."

"I don't think we should worry," said Olivia. "Ms. Primrose has promised to catch the person responsible."

"What if she doesn't, though?" Ava shot back. "It's been weeks since the sky-berry bushes were targeted, and no one's been caught yet. I'm going to ask my parents if they know of any plants that might help protect the academy." Ava's parents had a plant nursery.

"Good idea," said Sophia.

"And I'm going to keep reading books in the library to find any spells of protection that might be useful," said Layla.

"I'll help you," offered Olivia. She glanced at Isabel. "Do you want to help too?"

Isabel shrugged. "Maybe." Isabel was lucky that she found studying easy and could be at the top of the class with hardly any effort. But Isabel much preferred to be outside with Cloud, trying to discover his magic or having adventures, than sweating over her work! "Do any of you know where Scarlett and Blaze are?" she asked, seeing that her best friend wasn't with the others.

"I saw them trotting away with Billy and Lightning," said Sophia. "But I don't know where they went."

"I'll go and find them," said Isabel. "See you later."

Isabel and Cloud rode around the grounds

until Cloud stopped. "Can you hear that? That's Scarlett's laugh."

Isabel listened to the distant cheers and shrieks of laughter coming from near the orchard. "That's definitely Scarlett," she agreed. "Clever Cloud. Let's find out what she's doing."

Cloud whinnied with pleasure at the praise and broke into a canter. As they neared the orchard, Isabel inhaled the rich smell of magic. It always reminded her of burnt sugar. A second later she saw a trail of flames burning brightly in the air, then she spotted Scarlett and Blaze cantering in loops around the trees.

Billy and his unicorn, Lightning, watched from nearby, encouraging Blaze to perform more tricks.

"Ladies and gentlemen, it is time to give you the circle of fire!" yelled Scarlett, her blond hair flying out behind her and a huge smile on her face.

Blaze skidded to a halt and stamped a hoof. *Crack!* Sparks flared, and a large circle of flames hovered in the air before her.

"Drrrrrrrrrr!" Scarlett made the sound of a drum roll. The flames crackled and hissed. Blaze cantered forward and leaped neatly through the ring of fire.

Billy whooped, and Lightning stamped his hooves in approval.

"That's brilliant!" called Cloud.

Scarlett rode over, grinning. "Did you see that, Isabel? Blaze just jumped through—"

"A circle of fire," Isabel finished for her, feelings of jealousy curling in her tummy. "I know. I've seen you do that like a million times."

The smile dropped from Scarlett's face. "Oh," she said. "Well, we can try something else if you want."

Isabel felt guilty as she saw her friend's hurt face. Perhaps her words had been a bit harsh. "It's awesome that Blaze can do so much with her fire magic, but let's do something we can all join in with, like a race?"

"I'm in!" said Billy. "Race you back to the stables. Last one back is a dorky donkey!"

Billy and Lightning set off even before Billy had

finished speaking. Isabel leaned forward, shouting in Cloud's ear to urge him on. But Cloud wasn't the fastest unicorn, and there was no way he could catch Billy and Lightning or even Scarlett and Blaze unless . . .

"Take a shortcut through the picnic area. You can easily jump over the tables," whispered Isabel.

"You're joking?" panted Cloud. "Think of the trouble we'll be in if we're caught."

"Please, Cloud. I want to win!" begged Isabel.

Cloud hesitated and then suddenly swerved. "Okay. Just this once. For you."

Isabel laughed loudly, loving the rush of air on her face as Cloud galloped full speed toward the picnic tables.

"Hold tight," he whinnied as the first bench loomed closer.

Isabel hung on to his mane. Would such a huge leap help Cloud find his magic? What if he could

fly? Isabel's fingers curled even tighter around Cloud's mane. The ground seemed a long way down. She told herself she wasn't scared. The special island magic would keep her safe, forming a purple bubble around her to float her to the ground if she fell. But that didn't stop Isabel's stomach from twisting into a knot as Cloud soared way above the bench, landing with a thump and kicking up a clump of turf. He jumped again, even higher this time, clearing the second table with ease and galloping on toward the stables.

Isabel was breathless with excitement as they pulled up. "That was amazing," she panted, quickly forgetting her fright. "We won by miles!"

Isabel waited for Scarlett, Blaze, Billy, and Lightning to reach the stables.

"Well done!" cried Scarlett as Blaze arrived just after Lightning. "You won!"

"Cheater!" said Billy bitterly.

"You didn't say we couldn't take a shortcut," said Isabel, shrugging. "We won fair and square."

"All right," said Billy, rolling his eyes. "But next time we'll beat you."

"We'll see," said Isabel, sliding from Cloud's back. "Thanks, Cloud." She patted his neck and suddenly felt happier. "You're the best unicorn!"

Cloud nuzzled her hand. "And you're my *best friend*, Isabel," he said back.

CHAPTER 2

Isabel headed reluctantly into the classroom, still daydreaming about racing around on Cloud. She wished the geography lesson wasn't with Ms. Nettles, her least favorite teacher. Isabel found the work easy, but being top of the class wasn't enough for Ms. Nettles. She always gave Isabel extra tasks to do. On the way into the classroom Isabel almost collided with Ava, who was carrying a vase filled with three fluffy red flowers with long stems.

"Whoa! Sorry, Ava! Gosh, look at those monster flowers. Did you grow them? They're beautiful."

Ava smiled. "Yes. Peonies are supposed to bring good luck, so I'm going to put them in the classroom to bring us all luck in the drill ride this afternoon."

Isabel's heart lifted as she remembered that the first-year dormitories were competing against each other in a drill ride at teatime that day. In the competition, riders and their unicorns had to perform the same moves either together or one after another, with marks for how well the group did and for difficulty of routine. The drill ride was also being judged on presentation, with extra marks being awarded for the unicorns' tail and mane braids. They had been told that one person from each dormitory was going to be chosen as the leader. *I hope I'm the leader of Sapphire dorm,* Isabel thought.

"Keep those flowers on our side of the classroom," Isabel called to Ava as she carried the

peonies up to the front. If the flowers could bring good luck, then she wanted it to go to her own team!

Jacinta, from Emerald dorm, was sharpening pencils for Valentina. Valentina's parents were trustees, and she was also Ms. Nettles's niece. "I want them sharper than that!" she complained as she sat in her chair.

Jacinta nodded. "Of course, Valentina." She picked up a pencil to sharpen it further and then noticed Ava putting the flowers down on a windowsill. "Wow, Ava, they're lovely—"

"What, those silly weeds?" said Valentina, cutting across Jacinta and giving Ava a withering stare. "They stink, and my aunt will hate them."

18

Ava's smile vanished. Isabel reached Valentina's desk in an instant. "You're the one who stinks!" she said crossly. "You smell like frog poo!"

Valentina jumped to her feet. "How dare you! I use a very expensive shower gel! I'll tell my parents you've been rude."

Isabel rolled her eyes. "Oh, I'm SO scared!"

Just then Ms. Nettles came in carrying a pile of exercise books. She stopped and stiffened like a snake about to strike, her beady eyes flicking from Valentina to Isabel. "What's going on, girls?" she snapped.

"Isabel was being really mean to me, Auntie . . . I mean Ms. Nettles." Valentina's eyes widened. "She said really, *really* horrible things." Her voice rose in a wail.

"Isabel, I will not have bullying in my class!" said Ms. Nettles sharply.

"But—" protested Isabel.

"Sit down at once!" ordered Ms. Nettles.

"It wasn't Isabel's fault!" Ava jumped in quickly. "Valentina was being unkind."

"Atishoo!" Ms. Nettles sneezed, and her eyes started to stream. "For goodness' sake!" she exclaimed. "Someone remove those ridiculous flowers from over there before they kill me!" She pointed at Ava's peonies.

Valentina snorted with laughter. "Told you she wouldn't like them," she whispered as Ava grabbed the vase and carried it out of the class. Valentina rolled her eyes at Jacinta and Delia. "Ava's so dumb!" she sniggered as Ava passed their desks. They giggled as Ava turned bright red.

Isabel sat down next to Scarlett and glared at Valentina. "I'm going to get back at her for that," she muttered angrily. She hated it when Valentina was mean to Ava.

"Count me in," whispered Scarlett. "We'll plan something tonight!"

★

"Right, class, you may pack up now," said Ms. Nettles at the end of the lesson. "Ms. Rosemary is going to meet you in the stables, where you can start preparing your unicorns for the drill ride competition. However, first she wants me to tell you who will be leading each dormitory's team." Ms. Nettles unfolded the piece of paper.

Oh, please be me, please be me. Isabel crossed her fingers.

"Diamond dorm, your team leader will be Jason." Billy's friend Jason grinned and fist-bumped Billy and their friend Jack. Ms. Nettles's thin lips creased into a small, pleased smile. "Emerald dorm, your team leader is Valentina."

"Well, of course Ms. Rosemary chose me," said

21

Valentina, preening. "She knows I'm a natural leader."

"And Sapphire dorm . . ." Ms. Nettles's mouth pinched up as if she had just eaten a lemon. "Your leader is Isabel."

Isabel couldn't contain her excitement. She leaped to her feet with a whoop.

"Isabel!" snapped Ms. Nettles. "Will you please behave, for once? Now, off you go, everyone."

Isabel's heart sang. She was the leader and she was going to make sure her dorm won. "Come on," she ordered her friends. "The quicker we get to the stables, the more time we'll have to prepare."

Isabel already had a routine in mind. Leaving Layla to groom Cloud, she hurried to the outdoor school and set up two large jumps.

When the others joined her with their unicorns, Layla's eyes widened in surprise. "We're not jumping those fences in the drill ride, are we?" she said anxiously.

"Yes," Isabel told her.

"But I don't like jumping," said Layla, biting her lip.

"Don't be silly," said Isabel impatiently. "You have to jump, Layla. It's a drill ride, which means we all need to do the same thing if we want to get maximum marks." She noticed Ava and Sophia watching and whispering to each other. "Ava, Sophia, there's no time to chat," she said sharply. "If you mess around, we'll never win."

"So? I just want to have fun," said Sophia.

Ava and Olivia nodded in agreement.

"But it'll only be fun if we come in first," said Isabel. "So let's get on our unicorns and get practicing!"

That afternoon Isabel nearly shouted herself hoarse instructing the rest of Sapphire dorm. She was pleased with the results, especially after she decided they should add unicorn magic to the dance routine.

Rainbow made a rainbow slide for the others to ride over, and Star made flowers spring from the ground when they landed.

"That looks brilliant!" shouted Isabel to Dancer and Layla as they nervously cantered over the rainbow and landed in a bright cloud of petals. "The flowers are so pretty," she added, wishing that Cloud could show off some magic of his own in the drill ride.

Isabel had a huge smile on her face as the unicorns finished their routine, bowing together under a rainbow entwined with hundreds of flowers. But she was surprised to see how unhappy everyone else looked. "That was great fun, wasn't it? You all need to smile more," she told them. "I'm sure we'll get more marks for smiling. Now, let's go and get cleaned up. Ava . . ." Isabel's voice rose. "What have you done to your hands?"

Ava looked sheepish as she held out her blue hands. "It's dyer's knotweed. I'm growing it in my garden. The leaves give off a blue dye."

"Go and scrub it off," said Isabel. "And hurry up. There's only half an hour to get ready, and everyone has to look perfect!"

A little later, as Isabel led her spruced-up friends and their unicorns to the indoor school for the competition, she glanced over at the other teams. Thanks to all her instructions, Sapphire dorm and their unicorns were by far the neatest. The unicorns' coats shone, their manes and tails were immaculately threaded with glittering blue ribbons, and the girls had matching ribbons in their hair.

Ms. Primrose was judging with Ms. Rosemary and Ms. Nettles. Isabel's team was first, and their practice paid off. Everything went perfectly—even if Layla was as white as a sheet when she jumped.

In Isabel's opinion they were much better than the other teams, and it was no surprise to her when Ms. Rosemary pronounced them the winners and handed them a glittering silver trophy.

Isabel's eyes shone as she and her team cantered a victory lap around the arena. As they came out of the ring, she turned to high-five Scarlett, but Scarlett wasn't smiling.

"What's wrong?" asked Isabel. "You don't seem pleased that we won."

"I am, but . . ." Scarlett looked awkward. "You've upset some of the others."

"Who?" said Isabel in surprise.

"Well, everyone, because you were really bossy, but especially Layla. You know how much

she hates jumping, but you still made her do it."

Isabel was bewildered. "But she jumped the fences just fine. She needs to be braver."

Scarlett frowned. "Layla *is* brave. Remember how she was when the lake iced over? She went to the Frozen Wastelands with me to help unfreeze it even though she was really scared."

Isabel frowned. "So if she did that, she shouldn't mind doing a few jumps." She shrugged. "I think everyone should cheer up and be happy. We won. What else matters?"

"People's feelings matter too, Is," said Scarlett quietly.

Feeling fed up and slightly confused, Isabel pushed Cloud into a canter and headed for the stables. Halfway there, the sky darkened. A bolt of lightning hurtled from the sky, followed by an explosive *crack*.

"What was that?" shrieked Isabel.

"Thunder and lightning!" Cloud raced for cover as rain pinged from the sky, turning the ground into a muddy quagmire.

"Hurry," Isabel urged Cloud. They were almost home when she heard hooves coming up fast behind her.

"Slow down," shouted Isabel as Valentina and Golden Briar galloped past.

"Whoopsie, sorry!" yelled Valentina as Golden Briar's hooves plowed on, spraying Isabel and Cloud with muddy water. Her eyes glinted meanly, and she didn't look sorry at all.

Wet and grumpy, Isabel stomped around the stables, drying Cloud's coat, then giving him a bucket of sky berries for dinner. The rest of Sapphire dorm whispered together and glanced at her as they tended to their unicorns, and Isabel's irritation grew. Why weren't they more pleased that she had helped them win?

A thank you would be nice, she thought as she headed back to the dorm.

The heavy rain continued into the evening, the dark, gloomy summer sky echoing Isabel's mood.

After dinner, the girls of Sapphire dorm holed up in their lounge. Layla and Olivia read in the soft glow from the sapphire-jeweled lamps while

Ava and Sophia played cards. Isabel couldn't settle down and went to stand by the window, watching the rain coming down.

"Hey there," said Scarlett, coming over and slipping her arm through Isabel's.

"Hey," muttered Isabel. She still felt a bit cross with her.

"Do you have any ideas about pranks to play on Valentina yet?" asked Scarlett. "She's been strutting around like a peacock, telling everyone how she got you muddy."

"Has she?" Isabel raised her eyebrows.

Scarlett's eyes sparkled with mischief. "I think she definitely deserves to have a trick played on her."

Isabel nodded. "Hmm. Now, what are we going to do?"

31

CHAPTER 3

"I've got it!" exclaimed Isabel.

Looking across at Ava, she had seen that her hands were still faintly blue. Valentina often boasted that she had a really expensive shower gel that left her skin soft and beautiful. What if she added some of Ava's dyer's knotweed to it?

"Wouldn't it be funny if Valentina turned blue?" Isabel giggled as she shared her idea with Scarlett.

"That's brilliant!" said Scarlett, her eyes shining.

They sneaked outside into the rain to collect

some leaves from Ava's garden. Wearing gloves, they picked the leaves, squeezing the dye from them into a tiny bottle. Giggling quietly, Isabel and Scarlett tiptoed upstairs to Emerald dorm. It wasn't difficult to find Valentina's things. They were much grander than anyone else's. Shaking with laughter, Isabel added the blue dye to the posh gold tube containing Valentina's shower gel while Scarlett stood guard.

Not long after, when Isabel and Scarlett were lounging around in Sapphire dorm, they heard a shriek from the bathroom.

"My skin! Oh nooooooo! Look at me!"

Isabel and Scarlett exchanged looks and rushed to the corridor just in time to see Valentina running to Emerald dorm, blue legs and arms poking out from a huge bath towel.

Isabel and Scarlett burst out laughing.

Valentina continued to shriek as she stormed

down the hallway. "Jacinta! Delia! Get my aunt right NOW!"

Just then the bedtime bell rang. Isabel and Scarlett hurried back into their dorm, still giggling. The other four girls were sitting on Sophia's bed, talking about the mysterious incidents that had happened at the school.

"What's so funny?" asked Sophia as Isabel and Scarlett came in, but she didn't sound quite as friendly as she usually did.

"Nothing," said Isabel quickly. She'd tell everyone in the morning, once they'd gotten over the silly bad mood they'd all been in since the competition.

★

The next morning, Ms. Primrose asked Ava to stay behind after assembly. Isabel was wondering why, when she saw Valentina arrive in the classroom for her first lesson. Her arms and face were still streaked with blue! Isabel giggled.

"Hey, Valentina," she whispered. "Are you sure that shower gel of yours is working?"

Valentina hissed back, "This is Ava's fault, as you well know. Ms. Primrose is telling Ava off right now, and Ms. Nettles says if she plays any more tricks, then she won't be allowed to keep her garden."

"What?" Isabel stared at her in horror. "But it wasn't Ava's fault!"

"Who else would have done it?" snapped Valentina.

Isabel raced out of the classroom and ran all the way to the head teacher's office.

She didn't knock but just burst in. Ava was crying. "I did not expect this of you, Ava," Ms. Primrose was saying sternly.

"But I keep telling you, I didn't do it!" Ava protested.

Ms. Primrose swung around as Isabel barged in. "Isabel! Whatever is the meaning of this?"

"Please, Ms. Primrose, Ava didn't do anything to Valentina. It was me!" Isabel braced herself. She was going to be in a huge amount of trouble, but there was no way she was letting Ava take the blame.

Ava sent her a grateful look, and Ms. Primrose's face tightened. "I see," said the head teacher coldly, the usual twinkle absent from her eyes. "I apologize, Ava. You may return to class." Her icy glare fell on Isabel, who cowered slightly. "And you, Isabel, shall stay and explain your behavior."

Isabel tried her best to explain about Valentina being mean and wanting to get her back, but even to her own ears it sounded like a feeble excuse.

Ms. Primrose was angrier than Isabel had ever seen her before. "I also heard how you upset some of your dorm mates yesterday," she concluded. "You must work a lot harder at being both sensible and thoughtful, Isabel. You will not graduate from Unicorn Academy at the end of the year if you don't buckle down. Worse still, you could end up getting expelled. Do you understand me?"

"Yes, Ms. Primrose," said Isabel in a subdued voice.

"Good. Now, go back to class and don't let me hear one more bad thing about you, or you will be very sorry indeed," said Ms. Primrose sternly.

Isabel was very quiet as she returned to class.

Imagine spending a second year at the academy after her friends had left. Even worse, imagine if she was expelled! Isabel made a silent promise to behave better and work harder.

"Are you okay?" Scarlett whispered anxiously as Isabel apologized to Ms. Rosemary for being late, then sat down.

"Just about," muttered Isabel. She saw Ms. Rosemary's eyes fix on her and hastily opened her books. There was no way she was getting into more trouble today!

★

It rained all day and the following one. Outside lessons were canceled, and pupils weren't allowed to ride because the grounds were so muddy. The grayness of the sky reflected Isabel's mood. Although Ava had forgiven her for getting her into trouble, the other girls in Sapphire dorm, apart from Scarlett, were still keeping their distance.

After lessons on the second day, Layla, who had just finished reading yet another book on unicorn presentation, offered to show her friends how to do a triple tail braid. Isabel and Scarlett went along too, sharing a huge stripy umbrella as they walked to the stables.

"Look how high the water is," said Isabel as they passed Sparkle Lake. "It's almost overflowing the banks."

"It's not as sparkly as usual. It must be the mud," said Scarlett.

"It's going to flood the school if it keeps raining like this," said Olivia.

"I hope it's not an evil spell," said Layla anxiously. "What if someone is trying to cause trouble again?"

"Don't be silly, Layla. It's just rain," said Isabel, rolling her eyes.

"Layla's not silly. It could be a spell," said Sophia sharply.

Ava and Olivia nodded in agreement. Isabel bit her lip, feeling once again that her friends weren't very pleased with her.

Isabel found Cloud in his stall. He whickered when he saw her, his dark eyes lighting up in delight. Isabel felt a rush of warmth—at least he

was happy to see her. She threw her arms around his neck and hugged him.

Cloud nuzzled her. "Hello, Isabel. I'm glad you're here. It's boring staying in all day."

Isabel's heart swelled. Cloud might not be the most exciting unicorn, but he was loyal and he really did love her.

"I wish we could go out galloping, but we've been told to stay inside." Isabel grabbed a grooming kit and started to groom Cloud. But it wasn't long before her arm ached and she grew bored. Tossing the brush aside, she started on Cloud's mane and tail with a comb.

Layla walked around the stables, showing everyone how to do a triple braid. It was much harder than it looked, and before long, Isabel had her pretty pink ribbon in a tangle.

Luckily for Isabel, Scarlett came into Cloud's stable. "The rain's easing. Want to go outside?"

"Ooh, yes." Isabel threw her grooming brushes down.

Cloud and Blaze followed them into the courtyard.

"Where are you going?" asked Valentina as they passed Golden Briar's stable.

"None of your business," said Isabel.

Valentina's eyes narrowed. "Oh, really?"

Isabel and Scarlett ignored her.

"This feels great." Isabel spread her arms wide. "Let's do something fun. I know, let's play dares."

Scarlett's eyes sparkled. "Me first. I dare you to put your face in the drinking trough."

"Simple!" Isabel marched up to the trough and stuck her head in the water. She surfaced with a splutter, shaking water droplets from her hair. "Your turn now," she beamed as rainbow-colored droplets slid down her cheeks.

Scarlett didn't hesitate. She plunged her head

into the water trough and came up shaking like a wet dog, spraying Isabel.

"Eek!" Isabel shrieked with laughter.

"Call that a dare?" scoffed Valentina, coming outside with Golden Briar. She pointed at the clock tower on the stable roof and said, "I dare you to climb up there, Scarlett. Not you, Isabel," she added slyly. "It's far too high for *you* to climb."

"No, it's not!" Isabel ignored her pounding heart as she faced Valentina. "Nothing's too high for me."

Cloud gasped. "Ignore her, Isabel! That's too dangerous. I'm telling a teacher if anyone tries to climb up there."

"Cloud! You wouldn't!"

Cloud shook his silver-and-blue mane out of his eyes. "I will. It's too high."

"It is very high," murmured Scarlett.

"It's not that high. Watch and learn, Valentina!"

43

Isabel took off, leaping puddles as she raced to the clock tower door and yanked it open. She strode to the rope ladder and stared up at the internal mechanisms of the clock. A tingle of apprehension stirred inside her. The ladder was more rickety than she'd imagined and a lot steeper, but she couldn't back down now. Not with Valentina expecting her to chicken out.

"Here I go," she called in a voice that sounded braver than she felt.

"Isabel, stop!" Cloud stamped a hoof anxiously.

Isabel climbed quickly at first but slowed as the ladder creaked and swayed. The clock wasn't getting much closer. Isabel glanced down to see how far she'd come. Okay. That was far! She gripped the ladder more tightly.

"Isabel, come down," called Cloud. "Please!"

Isabel found she couldn't move. All she could think about was what would happen if she fell. *Look up, not down,* she reminded herself. She drew in a deep breath and slowly reached for the next rung. There. She'd gotten it; she was going to be fine. Isabel moved her foot higher, but she misjudged the distance and her foot slipped through the rung.

"Eeek!" she squeaked, gripping the ladder while her feet pedaled wildly in the air.

CHAPTER 4

Isabel hung on tightly as her feet frantically sought for a rung. She finally found it, and a relieved cheer rang up from below.

"Come down," said Scarlett. She sounded breathless. "The dare's off. Valentina and Golden Briar just cantered away."

Isabel was too scared to move again. "I'll be down in a minute," she squeaked, wishing her hammering heart would slow down. One minute passed, then two. . . .

"What are you waiting for?" called Scarlett.

Suddenly Isabel heard Cloud's voice.

"Don't worry, Isabel. I'm right here, just beneath you." His voice was calm and soothing.

Isabel swallowed and glanced down. The ground was a long way off, but she could see Cloud looking up at her. Her gaze met his, and some of the tension left her as she saw the reassurance in his eyes.

"I promise I'll catch you if you fall," said Cloud. "Come down slowly, one rung at a time."

Gradually Isabel unclenched her fingers and bravely moved a foot. She came down the ladder, rung by rung, hoping Scarlett and Blaze hadn't noticed her fear.

"That's it, you're almost on the ground," encouraged Cloud.

Isabel's heart slowed down to normal speed. Reaching the last rung, she stepped onto solid ground.

"I'm so glad you're safe!" Scarlett hugged her.

Cloud nuzzled her, breathing on her hair and whickering softly. "You did it! Well done."

Isabel threw her arms around Cloud's neck. "Thank you," she whispered so the others couldn't hear. "You really helped me up there."

Cloud breathed out happily. "That's what unicorns are for."

Burying her face in his mane, Isabel felt a wave of love hit her. Right then, she wouldn't have swapped Cloud for any of the unicorns in the academy. He was perfect!

"What is going on here?" Ms. Nettles's sharp voice rang out. Isabel, Scarlett, and the unicorns jumped guiltily and swung around. Ms. Nettles was striding toward them with Valentina and Golden Briar at her side, both looking unbearably smug.

"Um . . . nothing!" said Isabel quickly.

"Don't lie. I just saw you step off the ladder to the clock tower. Were you climbing it?"

"No," Isabel lied, trying to look innocent.

Ms. Nettles sucked in her cheeks and gave Isabel a disbelieving look. "I sincerely hope not. Climbing the clock tower would be irresponsible and dangerous and could lead to expulsion." She shook her head. "Hmmm, I'm not sure that you can be trusted to organize your free time sensibly, Isabel. See me after dinner in my study. I have several boxes of old books that need cataloging."

Isabel bit back a groan. Ms. Rosemary had organized an inter-dorm quiz after dinner. There was no point asking Ms. Nettles to reconsider. She had a reputation for extending a punishment if anyone dared to argue.

"Yes, Ms. Nettles." Isabel glared at Valentina, wishing she could turn her permanently bright blue. That would serve her right for deliberately getting her into trouble!

By the end of dinner the rain had turned heavy again. Isabel glanced out the window as she made her way to Ms. Nettles's study. The swollen lake had broken its banks. Its sparkly water, now dulled with mud, swirled across the lawn. Dread uncurled in her stomach. She'd ignored the others when they suggested that the rain might be someone trying to cause trouble for the school again, but what if they were right? Perhaps some sort of evil magic *was* causing the rain.

Ms. Nettles put Isabel straight to work in a small room next to her study. The box of books that

needed sorting was enormous. Isabel wished she had gloves as she sifted through the dusty, ancient books, discarding anything that was too moldy to be repaired. There was no chance of slacking off, as Ms. Nettles had left the door ajar and kept sticking her head through to check up on her.

A long while later, Isabel heard Ms. Primrose's voice next door. She sounded very serious. Isabel stopped work to listen.

". . . very concerned. Unicorn Academy seems to be in the grip of a malevolent spell, but for the life of me I can't work out which one. If this rain continues, the school will flood and I will be forced to send everyone home."

"No!" whispered Isabel in dismay.

"That would be very unfortunate," said Ms. Nettles.

"Indeed," said Ms. Primrose gravely.

The teachers talked for a little longer, then Ms.

Primrose left and Ms. Nettles came to tell Isabel she could go.

"I'll see you back here tomorrow, same time. Don't be late!"

"Yes, Miss," said Isabel, then she ran at full speed back to the dorm.

CHAPTER 5

Isabel's friends had just returned from the quiz and were chattering loudly as she burst through the shiny blue door.

"Listen!" Isabel jumped up and down on her bed to get everyone's attention. As silence fell, Isabel glanced around the room. The girls each had identical blue-and-silver duvets, a small wardrobe, and a chest of drawers with a sapphire-studded lamp. Everyone had personalized their area with posters, photographs, and trinkets. Isabel's heart beat frantically. *What if she had to leave all this and her friends behind?*

"Guess what I just overheard!" she said.

When Isabel finished, everyone spoke at once. Sapphire dorm was unanimous—not one of them wanted to be evacuated from the academy.

"It can't happen," said Olivia firmly. "Ms. P

will work it out. The whole of Unicorn Island is in danger if the academy closes and there's no one here to guard the lake."

There were murmurs of agreement.

Sophia lifted her chin. "I wish I knew who it was. I'd try to stop them."

"I bet it's the person in the black cloak," said Ava. Earlier that semester she and Sophia had been chased down the mountain by a cloaked figure riding a unicorn and firing spells at them.

"Me too," said Scarlett.

They all nodded and started to get ready for bed.

"So how was the quiz?" Isabel asked Scarlett, suddenly remembering that she'd missed it. "Did you win?"

"It was great fun—we came in third." Scarlett disappeared as she pulled her pajama top over her head.

"Third?" said Isabel, thinking she'd misheard. How could Scarlett think it had been fun if they'd only come in third?

"It was my fault. If I hadn't gotten my birds muddled, we'd have come in second." Sophia dissolved into giggles.

Ava continued the story. "Ms. Rosemary wanted the name of the bird that feeds on raspberry clams. It's a red bill, of course, but Sophia shouted out *red bum*. We laughed so much we missed the next two questions."

"Red bum?" said Isabel, raising her eyebrows. "I can't believe you said that, Sophia, and lost marks for the team."

"No one minded," said Sophia, shrugging.

"We were having too much fun," said Olivia.

Isabel frowned, bewildered. She sometimes felt she just didn't get her friends. How could losing a competition *ever* be fun?

It rained through the night and all of the following day. Rumors started to fly that the school was going to be evacuated. All of Isabel's free time was taken up sorting books for Ms. Nettles.

"It's a horrid job," she moaned to Scarlett as they parted company by the stairs. "The books are dusty and they stink."

Scarlett shuddered. "Ugh! Watch out for book beetles! My uncle had them, and they nibbled everything." Her eyes lit up. "If you find one, catch it and put it in Valentina's bed!"

Isabel reluctantly shook her head. "No way. I'm in too much trouble already. No more pranks for me."

Isabel worked quickly, putting the good books into one pile and the others into the bin. One dusty book with a dark green leather cover caught Isabel's eye. It was much thicker than the rest, and she needed both hands to lift it. As Isabel blew the dust away, she felt a tickle. A large brown beetle with yellow and black spots scuttled from the book and onto her hand.

"Ew! Get off!" Isabel tossed the book onto the floor, but the beetle clung to her hand, its antennae waving frantically.

"Eek!" Isabel accidentally kicked the book open as she danced about. The beetle scurried away, and Isabel bent to pick up the book. The pages were covered with small holes. Remembering what Scarlett had said about book beetles, she stared at the holes suspiciously. A chapter title leaped out at her: *Using Rain Seeds to Cause a Flood.*

A flood! Isabel glanced out the window, where the rain was pouring down, and her heart raced. Could the terrible rainstorm at the academy be caused by rain seeds?

She flipped to the right section and read on:

Rain seeds can be used to make rain fall. They are tiny blue pearls that can only be found in the deep sea. They are mostly used to create rain in areas suffering from a drought. However, they can also be infused with dark magic, which results in the rain becoming excessive.

If a stone is taken from a lake or river and placed with enchanted rain seeds next to an ocean, then excessive rain will fall continuously on the original lake or stream. This spell will work most effectively if the rain seeds are placed next to the ocean on the . . .

Here the page was covered with holes and crumpled from when Isabel had dropped and kicked the book. She skipped over it and continued reading.

To undo a dark spell, the rain seeds and the stone must be taken to the place of rain, put in

a puddle, and breathed on by a unicorn. The
bad magic will drain away, and the rain will
immediately stop.

Isabel read the passage again. The best ocean for the spell to work was where? She smoothed the paper, in the hope that she could read the rest of the sentence, when the page underneath rustled and another beetle jumped out. Isabel

yelped in surprise and let go. There was a ripping sound, and she was left holding the remains of the chapter on rain seeds in her hand.

Isabel stared at the torn pages in dismay. "Stupid beetle!" she cried. Now there'd be more trouble. Furious with the beetle for startling her and making her damage the book, Isabel swatted at it. "Go away, you horrible thing!"

As she did so, the study door opened.

"STOP!" Ms. Nettles stormed over. "Do not move a muscle!" she cried. "Stay right where you are!"

CHAPTER 6

Ms. Nettles dropped to her knees and began to frantically search the floor. "Whatever do you think you're doing?" she demanded.

"I'm sorry," Isabel stuttered, wondering why the teacher was crouching on the floor—and how much trouble she was going to be in. "I didn't mean to damage the book. There were beetles in it when I picked it up. They've nibbled holes in the paper."

Ms. Nettles's glasses were rattling so hard that Isabel expected them to slide right off her nose. She pointed a bony finger at Isabel. "Stay exactly where you are," she ordered as she continued to

63

search the floor. "Hester, Horatio, where are you, my lovelies? Come to Mommy."

For a moment Isabel thought the teacher had gone mad. It was only when Ms. Nettles found the two beetles and slipped them carefully inside a small box that Isabel realized what she was doing.

"They're *your* beetles?" she breathed.

"Yes! I collect them, but these two escaped when I was cleaning out their tank. If I *ever* catch you stamping on a beetle, you will be out of this school faster than you can say *unicorn*," said Ms. Nettles. "Hester and Horatio are the only two book beetles in my extensive beetle collection. They are also my favorites."

Ms. Nettles collected beetles. Weird! For a wild moment, Isabel wondered if Ms. Nettles might be the person trying to harm the lake. She was certainly odd enough. But that was a crazy idea. Why would a teacher do that?

"Your work here is done. I'll finish up. Go and wash your hands for dinner."

Isabel was only too happy to leave. "Thank you, Ms. Nettles. Please could I have that book back, though? I want to show it to Ms. Primrose."

"No," snapped Ms. Nettles. "Ms. Primrose is in a meeting and is far too busy to see you. I will deal with the damaged book."

"But this is important. There's a way of stopping the rain. . . ."

Ms. Nettles wouldn't listen. She tucked the book under her arm as she scooted Isabel out of her study. "Go!" she said, glaring down her nose. "If I hear any more of this nonsense about rain, you'll be in detention for the rest of the year. Is that clear?"

"Yes," sighed Isabel.

Ms. Nettles pulled a key from her pocket and locked the door. There was nothing Isabel could do but go.

On her way to the dining room, Isabel stopped to gaze at the rain coming down faster and faster outside. How could everything have gone so badly wrong? Six short months ago she'd stood in the hall bursting with excitement at the thought of meeting her unicorn. Now the academy might close before the year was over. Isabel wondered if everyone would be made to start the year again or

only the pupils and unicorns that still had to find their magic and bond. That would mean Scarlett and Sophia and Ava wouldn't come back and she'd be left with people like Valentina. No, that couldn't happen!

Isabel walked over to the rainbow-colored glass doors of the Great Hall and slipped inside. She wandered across to the magical map. It was a model of Unicorn Island surrounded by a magical force field that hummed softly. Isabel held out a finger and touched it curiously. "Ow!" She winced as it gave her a small electric shock.

The map had the power to take people anywhere on the island, but students were only allowed to use it with Ms. Primrose's permission. Staying clear of the force field, Isabel stared at the coastline. What if rain seeds *were* to blame for the rain? What if someone had hidden some on one of the island's coasts? She groaned inwardly.

If only she hadn't torn the book, then she would have known where to look.

Isabel recalled the words in the book. "This spell will work most effectively if the rain seeds are placed next to the ocean on the . . . ," she said. She looked at the map in frustration. "Which ocean? Where?"

"Talking to yourself?" said Scarlett, sneaking up behind her with the rest of the girls from Sapphire dorm. "What are you doing here? Haven't you heard? Ms. Primrose sent us to our dorms to pack. If it's still raining tomorrow, we're being sent home."

"What!" Isabel stared at her in horror. "But we can't leave. There might be a way to save the school! I think I know what's going on!" Isabel's words tumbled out as she told everyone about rain seeds.

Layla's face lit up. "Rain seeds!" she said,

banging her head with her hand. "Of course! I've read about them somewhere."

"Ava," Sophia piped up. "You're making your thinking face. What do you know about rain seeds?"

Ava blushed. "I don't actually know anything about rain seeds, but what if they behave in the same way as plants? Plants that need lots of water to flourish grow best in the west because it has the most rain. The incoming winds pick up water from the ocean, and it falls on land. If I had to guess, I'd say the rain seeds would work best if placed on the west coast, on or near cliffs to protect them from being accidentally kicked or stepped on."

"Really! I could go there!" said Isabel. Her face fell as she stared at the map. "But look how many cliffs are along the west coastline! It'll take an age to search there."

"And you have to ask permission to use the map," Olivia reminded her.

"How can I, when Ms. Nettles won't let me speak to Ms. Primrose?" Isabel's eyes hardened. "You know what? I'll go without asking."

"I'll come too," said Scarlett immediately.

Layla twisted a strand of hair around her hand. "And me."

"Me too." Ava, Sophia, and Olivia spoke together.

"Let's ask our unicorns along," said Scarlett. "We can cover more ground and go faster if we ride."

Isabel beamed at her brilliant friends. "You're on!"

Isabel's heart hammered as she ran to the stables. Her friends were keen to help, but what about Cloud? Would he think her plan reckless, especially after the clock tower incident, and stop her from going? She was breathless when she reached Cloud's stable and stuttered as she poured out her plan.

"Trust me, Cloud!" she begged. "Please say you'll come. I don't want to go without you." She realized she meant it. Cloud could be a little cautious sometimes, but she trusted him totally.

But to her delight, Cloud was already nodding. "Of course I'll come. We have to help the academy. You're right, Isabel, this is an emergency. And Ms. Primrose has just ridden away on Sage, so you can't ask her permission anyway!"

"Thank you." Isabel gave Cloud a grateful hug before jumping on his back and racing to the hall with her friends and their unicorns.

This time, as Isabel approached the map, the force field shone out brightly. Then, with a sudden flash, it disappeared, allowing Cloud to pass through. *It's as if the map knows we're trying to save*

the school, thought Isabel with an excited shiver. When everyone was lined up with her, Isabel said, "The west coast, then?"

"Yes," said Ava. "Definitely."

Isabel stared at the map one more time. It was a miniature version of Unicorn Island, with every single river, lake, mountain, stream, and building. Unicorn Academy was there too, its tiny lake overflowing, just like the real one. There wasn't a moment to lose.

"Everyone, hold hands," called Scarlett, who'd used the map before.

The girls linked hands, Isabel keeping one hand free to touch the west coast. She selected a beach with caves and a cliff, providing plenty of places to hide the rain seeds. Excitement surged through her as her fingertips touched the gritty sand. There was a burst of colored lights. A wind sprang up, whipping Isabel's curly hair around

her face. She was spinning, Cloud's mane blowing up as they spiraled faster and faster. Isabel clung to Cloud as he suddenly plummeted down.

CHAPTER 7

Cloud landed with a *whump*, his hooves sinking into soft ground.

Isabel opened her eyes and stared at her surroundings. The map had worked! She was in the middle of a sunny beach. The sea was a deep blue, and a salty breeze sent frothy waves licking at the shore.

"It's not raining here," said Scarlett, squinting up at the clear sky.

"It's lovely." Isabel stretched out her arms, letting the sun warm her. Her hand snagged on something caught in Cloud's mane.

"What's this?" she asked, holding up a tiny model of Unicorn Academy.

Scarlett grinned. "That's our way home. Don't lose it or we'll be galloping all the way back."

Isabel pushed the model deep down in her pocket. There wasn't time to ride back. They had to find the rain seeds and get them to the academy before everyone was sent away. She eyed the coastline stretching away in both directions, and then the caves and steep cliffs behind her. Her mind started to form a plan.

"It's going to take ages to find the rain seeds," she said, silently adding, *if they're even here.* "We should split up. Ava and Sophia, you take the beach. Olivia and Layla, you . . ." She was about to say *climb up and search the cliff paths,* but then she noticed that Layla was looking pale. Remembering how she'd felt when she'd climbed the clock tower, Isabel gave Layla the choice.

"Layla, would you prefer to search the cliff paths
or the caves?"

"The caves." Layla smiled gratefully.

"Okay, you two check the caves, and Scarlett
and I will go up the cliffs," said Isabel bravely.
"Good luck, everyone." She smiled encouragingly.
"We can do this. We can find the seeds!"

Isabel tried not to notice the height of the cliffs
as they set off. The sand stretched out invitingly in
front of them. "Let's gallop there!" she said. She
wanted to be the first to find the seeds.

But Cloud slowed down to a walk. "I don't think we should. The ground feels spongy—there might be sinking sand."

"But—" said Isabel.

"We won't find the seeds if we get stuck," interrupted Cloud.

Isabel fell silent. Cloud had a good point. She let him set the pace and concentrated on scanning the cliffs, hoping to see somewhere that rain seeds might be hidden.

As Cloud and Blaze started up the steep cliff

path, Isabel wound a lock of Cloud's silvery-blue mane around her hands for courage. When Isabel saw a flash of blue from under a bush, Cloud left the path to investigate.

The cliff face was steep, with loose stones, and Isabel clung on tightly as Cloud inched forward. Suddenly he lost his footing and slid several yards down before a scratchy bush broke his fall. Isabel's heart banged wildly against her ribs. The island magic would stop her from falling off, but would it protect Cloud from falling down the cliff?

"I'm fine," gasped Cloud, sensing Isabel's worry. He edged up to where she had seen the flash of blue, but she was disappointed to see it

was just a blue stone hidden by some golden flowers.

They went on a bit farther, and Scarlett spotted something blue in a hollow. Isabel held her breath as Blaze walked sideways across the cliff face to reach it. Scarlett slid from his back and stuck her arm in the hole.

"She's found them!" Isabel was so relieved the seeds had been found that she realized she didn't care that it was Scarlett who had gotten to them first. But her relief was cruelly dashed when Scarlett held up a blue feather.

"Not the seeds," said Scarlett ruefully.

Undeterred, they continued the search.

At the top of the cliff, Cloud said they should turn back. "The rain seeds won't be up here. I've got a really strong feeling that Ava's right—they need to be closer to water."

Isabel looked back at the path they'd taken along the crumbly cliff face. She bit her lip, butterflies fluttering in her tummy at the thought of the journey down.

"Don't worry," said Scarlett, mistaking her

concern. "The others might have found the seeds."

When they reached the beach, Isabel saw that the tide had turned and big waves were rolling in toward the bottom of the cliffs. Ava and Sophia were tiny specks in the distance.

"The sand's firm here—we can gallop if you want," Cloud said to Isabel.

"Race you to catch up to them," said Scarlett, pushing Blaze into a gallop.

"We haven't found them yet," Sophia called to them as they rode up to her and Ava.

"Let's go and help Olivia and Layla," said Isabel. Shielding her eyes from the sun, she looked at the caves. "There they are—see that tall rock jutting out into the sea? There's a cave at the bottom. I can just see Dancer's tail."

"Watch out for the sinking sand," called Cloud anxiously. "There are patches all around here."

"How can you tell?" Blaze asked him.

Cloud looked surprised. "I can just feel it with my hooves. It feels wetter than normal sand. Can't you feel it too?"

"No," said Blaze.

Cloud pawed the ground, and for a moment Isabel thought she saw a faint pink spark flicker into the air. She frowned. Was there really a spark? But no. It had gone. She focused her mind on the important thing—reaching Olivia and Layla.

"Everyone follow Cloud," instructed Isabel. "It'll be safer."

The others fell into line behind Cloud and followed as he picked his way sure-footedly around the patches of sinking sand.

"Look at the sea," said Scarlett suddenly. "It's coming in really fast. Olivia, Layla!" she shouted. "Get out of the cave. Now!"

Isabel felt a shiver run down her spine as she

realized Scarlett was right. Long fingers of water were curving around either side of the caves, and huge waves were breaking on the rocks.

"Olivia, Layla, you have to leave!" Isabel shouted desperately. "They can't hear us. If they stay in the cave any longer, they won't get out. We've got to warn them! Cloud and I will go."

"We're coming too," said Scarlett.

The incoming waves swirled around Blaze and Cloud, pushing and pulling at their legs.

"Hang on, Scarlett!" shouted Blaze, stumbling.

Scarlett slid onto Blaze's neck. With shaking hands, she pushed herself upright.

"Enough!" said Isabel. "You two stay here. Cloud and I are going on alone."

"No way . . . ," Scarlett began to protest.

Isabel's mouth set in a determined line. "It's too dangerous, and it's silly for us all to take a risk. Cloud is best at working out where the sinking sand is, so you have to let us go." She urged Cloud on, and he splashed into the water and headed for the cave entrance.

The waves quickly covered his fetlocks and then his knees, reaching up to his belly. Isabel cried out as a wave broke against them and Cloud staggered. His mane was sticking to his neck like silvery-blue seaweed. Isabel's legs were drenched. She could see Olivia and Layla just inside the cave entrance. They had clearly noticed the water and were trying to get out but realized they were trapped. She could hear Dancer and Snowflake whinnying over the roar of the incoming sea.

Cloud struggled to stay on his feet as the waves smacked into them again. "It's no use," he shouted. "We'll have to go back to the academy and get the teachers to help."

"There isn't time," protested Isabel. "We have to help them out, Cloud. If we don't, they're going to drown!"

CHAPTER 8

"What are we going to do, Isabel?"

Isabel sensed Cloud's panic. The unicorn trembled as a wave almost knocked him over.

"I'll think of something," she said, trying to keep calm despite the fear that was rising inside her as she listened to her friends' shouts for help. "The waves are strong, but maybe we can still get to them and help them get out."

Cloud hesitated. Isabel wrapped her arms around his neck and hugged him tightly. "We can do this, Cloud. Trust me!"

The hug seemed to rally Cloud. Staring intently

at the sea, he took a step toward the cave and then another, pushing his legs through the swirling water as it rose higher and higher. With each step, his confidence seemed to return.

Isabel urged him on. "That's it, Cloud. Keep going!"

Suddenly she noticed something strange. The sea seemed to be moving away from Cloud's hooves.

"Cloud, are you doing that?" she demanded.

Cloud looked to where Isabel was pointing. "Y-yes, I think I am. I was just thinking about the sea parting to let me through and . . . and it seems to have happened!" he said in astonishment.

"Try it again," said Isabel.

Cloud strode forward.

Isabel felt something crackling in the air. It was accompanied by the rich smell of burnt sugar. Isabel recognized the smell instantly. Magic! All

of a sudden there was a sound like paper ripping, and the sea divided, opening up like a long zipper.

"Cloud!" squeaked Isabel as a path of wet, shining sand appeared before them, leading straight to the cave. "Look what you've just done!"

Cloud didn't answer. Isabel could tell he was concentrating hard as he used his water magic to hold the sea back.

Olivia and Layla, on Snowflake and Dancer, came slowly out of the cave. They looked around in astonishment, staring at the sea that was being held back on either side of them, two looming blue walls of water.

"Hurry," gasped Cloud. "Get to safety! I haven't got the strength to hold the sea back for long!"

"Go that way!" Isabel shouted, pointing to where the tide was coming in more slowly. If they could reach the base of the cliffs, they could follow a path that led up to the cliff top, where the others were anxiously waiting.

The unicorns didn't need any more urging—they cantered through the water, heading toward the cliff path. Cloud whinnied and charged after them. As he galloped down the sandy path, the sea walls collapsed behind him. Isabel urged him on, stroking his neck. "You're amazing, Cloud! You're

the best unicorn ever!" She felt new strength surge through Cloud, and he galloped faster than he ever had in his life, his tail streaming out like a banner behind him.

At last all the girls reached the cliff and scrambled up the path to where the sea couldn't reach them. Then Isabel felt Cloud's legs wobble, and he collapsed on the ground, his sides heaving. Isabel slid from his back.

"Oh, Cloud, you were fantastic." She threw her arms around him and buried her face in the unicorn's soaked neck. "Are you okay?"

"I've found my magic," said Cloud, sounding dazed. "I can control water. I can part the tide and the waves. I bet I can even make it rain."

"Don't make any more rain!" said Scarlett in alarm.

Cloud managed to laugh despite gasping for breath. "No more rain. I promise." He turned to

Isabel and nuzzled her. "You helped me find my magic, Isabel. Thank you."

Isabel was filled with a glow that fizzed right through her, and her brain raced as she thought of all the amazing things she and Cloud could do with his newfound water magic. She hugged him, and he tried to stand but his legs gave way beneath him. "I'm sorry," he gasped. "I'm sure I'll be okay in a minute."

Layla seemed worried. "You look exhausted, Cloud. Parting the sea must have used up all your energy."

"I'll be fine," Cloud said bravely. But although he tried again, he still couldn't stand.

Isabel looked anxiously at Layla. She knew the most about unicorns. "What can we do?"

"We need something to give him strength," said Layla. "We really need sky berries or water from Sparkle Lake."

"But we haven't got those," said Isabel. Cloud's muzzle sank down on the ground and his eyelids flickered. She couldn't bear it. He had been so brave. They had to find a way to help him. "Isn't there anything else we can do?"

"There's a plant called Unicorns' Gold that gives unicorns strength," Ava said. "It grows on cliffs near the sea."

Isabel frowned as she remembered something. "What does it look like?"

"The flowers are gold with five petals and a silver center," said Ava.

"I saw some flowers like that earlier!" Isabel burst out, thinking of the flowers she'd seen on the cliff. "They were over there." She pointed across the cliffs to where she and Scarlett had been searching.

"We can't get over there now because of the tide," said Scarlett.

"Don't worry. If there was some Unicorns' Gold there, then there is very likely to be some near here too," said Ava. "These are the perfect growing conditions for it."

"Up there!" gasped Sophia, squinting and pointing to a ledge high above them. "I can see some gold flowers! Is that Unicorns' Gold, Ava?"

Ava followed her gaze. "It could be."

"I'll go and find out," said Isabel.

"Be careful!" gasped Cloud.

Isabel scrambled up the cliff path and started to climb out onto the cliff face toward the ledge where the flowers were. Halfway up, Isabel looked back at the others. There was a dizzying drop beneath her, and there was still a long way to go. But even from here, she could see Cloud's sides heaving. Isabel turned back. *I don't want to do this,* she thought, her palms starting to sweat. *But I have to. I can't let Cloud down.*

Slowly, she clambered upward, stopping several times as she searched for the next handhold. Once, she accidentally looked down and froze, her heart skittering at the enormous distance to the ground.

"You can do it!" Scarlett's voice floated up to her. "Keep going!"

"Go on, Isabel!" gasped Cloud.

The other girls shouted encouragingly, and the unicorns whinnied, urging Isabel on.

Isabel breathed deeply until her heart slowed and her legs stopped trembling quite so badly. Reaching up for the next handhold, she determinedly hauled herself up to the ledge.

"Made it!" Isabel sat with her back to the rock face. The view was amazing, even if it made her feel extremely squiggly inside. She looked at the flowers—they were just as Ava had described: five gold petals with a silver center. It must be Unicorns' Gold! She began to pick handfuls and

stuff them in her pockets. Suddenly her fingers brushed against something that sent a tingle up her arm.

"What's that?" Isabel parted a clump of flowers, and her mouth opened in surprise. Hidden in the middle, she found a large stone and five blue pearls! Her heart flipped in her chest.

"The rain seeds!" she shouted to the others in astonishment. "I've found the rain seeds!"

Whoops and cheers floated up to her from below, and the unicorns whinnied as Isabel put the rain seeds and the stone, which she guessed must have come from Sparkle Lake, in her pockets, along with the handfuls of Unicorns' Gold.

Climbing back down to the path was much easier. As soon as she reached the others, she gave some flowers to Cloud. He ate them eagerly, and she shared the rest. The other unicorns gobbled them up.

Cloud's velvet-soft lips gently nuzzled her fingers. "That feels so much better!"

"I feel stronger," said Dancer.

"And faster," said Star.

"I can stand again," said Cloud. He got up and raised his nose to Isabel's face, breathing out gently. "Thank you, Isabel. It was incredibly brave of you to climb up there."

Isabel hugged him. "You're the brave one. You fought through the water and found your magic power."

"I couldn't have done it without you," said Cloud.

"And I couldn't have done any of this without you," said Isabel, thinking how much she had learned in the last few days. She glanced around at her friends and their unicorns. She was beginning to understand why the others hadn't minded when they lost the dormitory quiz. Working with friends and being part of a team was as good as winning, and sometimes even better!

She kissed Cloud's forehead. "Thank you."

"Enough with the soppy kissing! If Cloud is better, we should go," said Scarlett with a huge grin. "You need to use the model of the academy. It will take us home."

Isabel vaulted onto Cloud's back. Taking the

miniature Unicorn Academy from her pocket with one hand, she reached out to Scarlett with the other. "Hold hands, everyone," she instructed.

The tiny Unicorn Academy sparkled brightly, and Isabel felt the magic as it thrummed against her hand.

"We want to return to Unicorn Academy, please."

A strong wind sprang up. Isabel gasped as it rushed around her and then whisked her and her friends up in the air. Isabel's hair flew everywhere, and she shut her eyes as the wind spun her around and around. The spinning stopped suddenly. Then Isabel felt herself fall. With a gentle bump, Cloud landed.

They were outside the academy. As Cloud started to gallop around the back of the school to the lake, Isabel noticed that her hand was

empty. The tiny Unicorn Academy building had disappeared.

Cloud and the other unicorns pulled up at the lake, skidding to a halt in a spray of dark mud.

"Not a moment too soon," said Isabel, pointing at the tide of murky water oozing over the grass toward the academy. The rain was still falling, and the lake had overflowed its banks.

The girls dismounted and everyone formed a circle. Isabel looked at the soggy grass. There were plenty of puddles to choose from. Selecting the nearest, she placed the rain seeds and the stone in the middle and stood back. "It's up to the unicorns now," she explained. "The bad magic can only be removed from the water when a unicorn breathes on the rain seeds and the stone. On the count of three: one, two, three. . . ."

The unicorns blew together, sending a long draft of sweet-smelling breath over the rain seeds.

The seeds glowed bright blue until each one emitted a loud *pop*, then fizzled away to nothing.

In the silence that followed, the rain stopped. The puddles retracted and the water seeped back into Sparkle Lake, which now shimmered brightly with every color imaginable in the suddenly strong summer sunshine. A triple rainbow appeared over the lake, its graceful arches sparkling.

"We did it!" cried Isabel.

"Isabel," squeaked Scarlett. "Look—your hair!"

Isabel pulled at a curl and saw that it had turned silver and blue, the same color as Cloud's mane.

"We've bonded," she whispered in delight. "Look, Cloud! We've actually bonded."

Isabel beamed as she led Cloud down to

the lake for a well-earned drink of the magical water. The others followed, and when they were full, Cloud dipped his hoof in the lake and then stood back. A split second later, a fountain of water rose up from the lake, spraying everyone.

"Eek!" Isabel squealed with delight as Cloud continued to play, creating huge waves and fountains and even making it rain on the girls until everyone was soaked again.

Isabel was having so much fun, she didn't notice Ms. Primrose cantering toward them on Sage. Cloud had just created a tunnel through the lake, and Scarlett had stepped beneath its watery roof when Cloud heard Ms. Primrose shout. He let the tunnel collapse, drenching Scarlett and Blaze with glittering water.

Isabel's stomach tightened. "Now I'm in for it," she muttered. "Gosh, Ms. P does look angry. I hope she's not going to expel me for breaking so many rules, especially using the magic map without permission."

"Isabel," said Ms. Primrose sharply. "Girls! What are you doing?"

Cloud began to tremble. "Don't let her send you away, Isabel. I couldn't bear it if we had to part."

"I won't!" said Isabel fiercely, hugging him. "Whatever happens, nothing's going to separate us. You're the most perfect unicorn in the world."

She stepped forward, feeling the sun already drying her wet clothes. "I'm sorry, Ms. Primrose. This is my fault, all of it. Please don't expel anyone else. I talked them into helping me with everything, including using the map, but I couldn't sit back and let the academy close. Oh, and if you do expel me, I'm taking Cloud with me. We've bonded, and I won't go anywhere without him!"

Ms. Primrose looked angrily around the group, taking in each and every one of the girls and their unicorns. "Well," she said. "I really think I should expel you all. . . ."

Isabel felt a rush of sickness at Ms. Primrose's words. Did she mean it or was she joking? She certainly looked angry. Then Isabel suddenly became aware of the sound of hooves. To her amazement, she saw the teachers riding their unicorns at a fast gallop toward her. Ms. Nettles was in the lead, and she stopped just short of Isabel and Cloud.

"It's stopped raining." Ms. Nettles held out a tiny scrap of paper to Isabel. "You did this, didn't you? I found this after you'd been sorting out those books. I could just make out a few words: *rain seeds* and *west coast*. You found a way of stopping the rain. I'm proud of you, Isabel. I was beginning to think that you'd never buckle down and make use of that super-smart brain of yours."

"Quite," said Ms. Primrose, sounding flustered. "You shouldn't have used the map without my permission, and you certainly shouldn't have left the academy without telling anyone. But I'm glad you did, girls, and of course none of you shall be expelled!" Her eyes held Isabel's and then she smiled. "Your quick thinking and bravery today have saved not just Unicorn Academy but the whole of Unicorn Island. The rain seeds were contaminated with very bad magic. Whoever did that clearly hopes to gain control of the lake and the magical rivers of Unicorn Island. We must all continue to be vigilant."

"We will. We promise." Isabel couldn't stop smiling. They'd saved the island!

"Take your unicorns back to the stables, then go and unpack your suitcases," said Ms. Primrose. "After dinner, I'll hold a special inter-dorm competition to celebrate your achievements today."

Isabel was so happy, she felt like she was floating as she rode back to the stables on Cloud, beneath a clear blue sky. The feeling continued as she brushed him down and then went to the feed room to collect his evening meal of sky berries. On the way to Cloud's stable, Isabel heard someone shout her name.

"Hey," said Scarlett, lobbing a damp sponge

at her. "You're miles away. I bet you're plotting dorm domination at the competition tonight!"

"I wasn't, actually." Isabel threw the sponge back, chuckling as it splattered against Scarlett's shoulder. "I was thinking how silly my friends are and how we'll probably lose because someone from Sapphire dorm will shout out *red bum* or *unicorn poo!*"

"Oh! We heard that."

Suddenly, wet sponges were flying at Isabel from all directions.

"Joke!" she squealed, hurling them back. "Cloud, help! You're a water unicorn. Save me!"

With a clatter of hooves, Cloud came to the rescue, using his magic to turn the water in the drinking trough into a fountain and spray everyone, including Isabel. They squealed and shrieked until he stopped.

"Saved you!" he said to Isabel, his eyes shining.

Isabel shook off the water and flung her arms around Cloud's neck. "Yes," she said, her heart feeling as if it would burst with happiness. "You really did."

Layla's unicorn, Dancer, is afraid of riding fast and jumping high. When the trees around Sparkle Lake start to die, can Layla and Dancer be brave and look for a cure?

Read on for a peek at the next book in the Unicorn Academy series!

The sun shone on the marble towers of Unicorn Academy as Layla ran to the stables. She couldn't wait to show her beautiful unicorn, Dancer, the new sparkly hoof polish that had arrived from her parents. She planned to brush his velvety coat and then paint his hooves.

Layla had loved unicorns for as long she could remember. It had been a dream come true when, just after her tenth birthday, she'd traveled with her parents across Unicorn Island to become a student at Unicorn Academy. On their first day at the academy, students were paired with their

very own unicorn. Each pair spent the next year working together and learning to trust each other so that they could bond and graduate to become guardians of Unicorn Island.

Layla had been delighted when Ms. Primrose, the wise head teacher, had paired her with Dancer. He was very handsome, and had a snow-white coat. But Layla loved him most for his kind, thoughtful nature. He was perfect!

I'm so lucky, she thought as she reached the stables. Being at Unicorn Academy was amazing. It wasn't just because she had a unicorn of her own; she also loved the lessons and, although she'd felt quite shy at first, she'd made friends with the five other girls in Sapphire dorm.

The stables' shiny automatic trolleys full of hay trundled down the aisle in front of her as she walked in. Layla called out, "Good morning!"

but there was no reply. The stalls that the Sapphire dorm unicorns slept in were empty. As it was such a lovely morning, Layla decided the unicorns must have gone out to play. She hurried back outside and found them gathered beside a rainbow-colored stream that ran through the meadow. All the streams and rivers in the land contained water that flowed from Sparkle Lake, the huge magical lake in the school grounds. The water was very important because it nourished the people and the land and strengthened the unicorns' magic.

Layla paused. All the Sapphire dorm unicorns—Dancer, Blaze, Rainbow, Star, Cloud, and Snowflake—were standing on one bank of the wide stream.

"I bet you can do it, Dancer!" said Rainbow, tossing his brightly colored mane.

"You're the best at jumping," said Star.

"Go, Dancer! Go!" chanted Blaze, stamping her front hooves, her fire magic making sparks fly into the air.

Each unicorn had their own magic power that they discovered while they were at the academy. Dancer still hadn't found his magic yet. Layla hoped it would be something like healing magic. It would be lovely to be able to make people well again. She definitely wouldn't want him to have something scary like fire magic!

She watched as Dancer reared up on his hind legs. He balanced for a moment and then rushed forward. Galloping toward the stream, he leaped into the air, soaring across the water with the grace of an eagle. He landed safely on the far side of the bank, and the other unicorns all whinnied.

"You're so good at jumping!" called Cloud admiringly.

Dancer's eyes shone with the praise, and Layla's heart sank. Dancer was brilliant at jumping and Layla knew how much he enjoyed it, but she hated galloping fast and jumping and avoided both at all costs.

"The rest of us will never be able to jump that far," said Star.

Rainbow's eyes sparkled. "Then I guess we'll have to use magic to get across!"

He tossed his mane, and multicolored light shone from the center of his forehead. It arched across the stream, forming a rainbow bridge. Rainbow anchored the light to the ground. Whinnying happily, the unicorns galloped across it and surrounded Dancer.

Layla hesitated and then, shoving the hoof polish into her pocket, headed back to school. She'd let Dancer have some fun with his friends. She could paint his hooves another time.

"Layla! Wait!"

There was the sound of hooves cantering up behind her. It was Dancer. "Were you looking for me?" He pushed his nose against her chest. She stroked him, happiness spiraling through her as she breathed in his sweet smell—a mixture of hay and sky berries.

"I was. I've got some new hoof polish, but you look like you're having fun." Layla hugged him. "Go and finish your game. I can paint your hooves later."

"The game's finished. Did you see me jump the widest part of the stream?" He nuzzled her, and she took out the polish. "Gold and silver! That's fancy! Should we go to the stables and try it out?"

"I really don't mind if you want to stay here," said Layla.

"I'd rather be with you." Dancer's eyes met hers.

Layla smiled, and they walked back to the stables, her hand on his neck. Dancer was totally selfless and very loving. She just wished she could be a better friend to him—she knew he would love her to go galloping and jumping with him.

As her fingers played in his mane, she wondered when they would bond. She would know when it happened because a lock of her hair would turn the same color as his mane. If she was being

honest, she was a bit surprised it hadn't happened already. Four of the six girls in her dorm had already bonded with their unicorns. But maybe it would happen when Dancer finally discovered his magic. A worrying thought crept into her brain— maybe he wouldn't discover his magic, and they wouldn't graduate at the end of the year.

Most students just spent one year at the academy, but those who hadn't bonded with their unicorns, or whose unicorns hadn't discovered their magic by the end of the first year, stayed on for longer. Layla didn't mind the thought of staying on at the academy, but it would be strange if all her friends graduated and she didn't.

"Look, there's Ms. Primrose," said Dancer.

Layla followed his gaze. The head teacher was cantering her majestic unicorn, Sage, across the school grounds toward the gates. Sage's mane and tail were flying out behind him, shining pure

gold in the sunlight. It was rumored that he was related to the first unicorns who ever lived on Unicorn Island.

"I wonder where they're going," said Layla, seeing that Ms. Primrose was wearing a backpack. "I hope everything's okay."

Unease trickled down her spine. Sinister things

had been happening at the academy. First, Sparkle Lake had been polluted. Then a nasty spell had caused the lake to freeze. And Layla knew the teachers suspected that dark magic had caused the sky-berry bushes that grew near the school to die. Sky berries were essential for the unicorns' health, and the unicorns' magic had already begun to fade by the time Ava found new sky-berry bushes in the mountains. Then there'd been torrential rainfall that caused the lake to flood and almost shut the school down. Layla and her friends in Sapphire dorm had saved the lake each time, and Ms. Primrose had been very grateful. However, so far the culprit hadn't been caught. It was horrible to think of someone trying to harm the unicorns and the lake. Layla couldn't understand why anyone would do that.

"Layla! Watch out!" a voice snapped.

Layla jumped and stopped walking. She'd been

so deep in thought that she had almost bumped straight into Ms. Nettles, the Geography and Culture teacher. Ms. Nettles glared down her pointy nose at Layla, her sharp eyes cross behind her glasses.

"Walking along with your head in the clouds, Layla! That isn't like you."

"Sorry, Ms. Nettles."

"Just look where you're going in the future. Now, out of my way. Ms. Primrose has been called to an urgent meeting and left me in charge."

"Is the meeting about the bad things that have been happening here?" Layla knew from her parents' letters that everyone on Unicorn Island was beginning to worry.

Ms. Nettles frowned. "That's none of your concern. If you've nothing better to occupy your time, then I've some empty beetle cages that need cleaning."

"Sorry, Ms. Nettles, but I've got something really important to do," said Layla, hastily diving into the stables with Dancer.

Ms. Nettles collected beetles, and although Layla found all the animals and insects on the island interesting, she didn't want to clean out some smelly old cages. Luckily, Ms. Nettles didn't pursue her but strode off toward the school, stopping briefly to pat her unicorn, Thyme, on the way.

"So you think Ms. Primrose's meeting has something to do with all the things that have been going on?" asked Dancer.

"I don't know," said Layla. "Maybe something else bad has happened that only the teachers know about."

Dancer nuzzled her. "If that's the case, then we'll have to work together to try to protect the academy and the lake like we've done before."

Layla nodded. "Yes," she said firmly, feeling fear curl in her tummy at the thought. She really didn't like adventures but wanted to protect her school. Her brown eyes shone with determination. "We'll do whatever it takes."

PuRRmaiDs

Meet your
newest feline
friends!

PuRRmaiDs 1
The Scaredy Cat
Sudipta Bardhan-Qua

PuRRmaiDs 2
The Catfish Club
Sudipta Bardhan-Quallen

#1277   RHCBooks.com   RHCB